MEL BAY PRESENTS
CLIFTON CHENIER

THE KING
OF
ZYDECO

transcribed by
Gary Dahl

This book is available either by itself or packaged with a companion audio and/or video recording. If you have purchased the book only, you may wish to purchase the recordings separately. The publisher strongly recommends using a recording along with the text to assure accuracy of interpretation and make learning easier and more enjoyable.

FOREWORD

Clifton Chenier will always be known as the King of Zydeco. Although he didn't invent the form, he popularized it around the world by combining the most vital elements of Creole, Cajun, and blues music, all of which he heard as a young boy in his native Louisiana, into his own unique and intensely original musical gumbo. With a shout of "Laissez les bon ton roulet!" ("Let the good times roll!") he took his music far beyond the confines of his home region, first to Louisiana expatriates along the Gulf Coast and in California, to blues and R&B fans across the country, and eventually to young lovers of pop and rock music throughout the world who had never heard the term "zydeco" before him.

Chenier's mastery of his instrument and the power of his music and vocals have virtually defined the genre's repertoire, sound, and instrumentation. Looking at the hundreds, or perhaps thousands, of zydeco bands around the world, one would be hard-pressed to find a group that didn't acknowledge their great debt to him or perform a large number of his compositions in the basic style he came to define. In that way Clifton Chenier is to zydeco as Bill Monroe is to bluegrass music or James Brown to funk and soul.

As an accordionist, Clifton Chenier broke new ground by combining all the various elements of Louisiana's regional styles with R&B, even rock n' roll, and playing them on a piano accordion, very different from the more traditional Cajun use of the button accordion. But play it he did, with incredible power and conviction. His sound was steeped in the Creole tradition and dripped with blues. His use of the accordion as the centerpiece of a jumping, rocking band has done much to fuel the current resurgence in interest in the accordion and pull the instrument about as far away from its "Lady of Spain" stereotype as possible!

To understand zydeco accordion, you must understand Chenier's playing. Here's where it all began, and these transcriptions of many of his finest recordings for Arhoolie Records will show you in detail just what he played to make the wonderful sounds he is so famous for. As you study these transcriptions, you should also listen to the Clifton Chenier recordings of these songs. There are limits to what notes, rests, and measures can communicate on the printed page; and, to fully grasp the essence of Clifton Chenier, you must hear his music. All of the selections in this book are from recordings on Arhoolie records. Arhoolie also produced a 60-minute video, *Clifton Chenier – The King of Zydeco* (Arhoolie video 401), with concert footage. interviews, and television appearances, which allows you to study his technique and performing style up close. Both the recordings and the video are highly recommended.

Clifton Chenier was born on June 25, 1925, near Opelousas, Louisiana. His father, Joseph, in addition to being a farmer, was an accordionist who played waltzes, two-steps, and other traditional dances of the region at local house parties and gatherings. As a child, Clifton heard mostly "French" music, a hybrid of Black and White, Creole and Cajun music, live and on record. It's no wonder that the music he eventually made his own was a combination of these and several other styles. He recalled hearing recordings by one of zydeco's pioneers, African-American accordionist Amede Ardoin (Arhoolie/Folklyric CD 7007), who played and sang traditional and original material with a definite bluesy edge. As Clifton matured, he found himself drawn more and more to music and the accordion.

Chenier helped support the family by working in the rice, cotton, and sugar cane fields. Music was always an interesting and satisfying hobby, but hard physical labor brought in the money to survive. By 1946, he and his older brother, Cleveland, who would later play an important role in defining the rhythmic components of classic zydeco music with his wonderful rubboard playing, were working in Louisiana oil refineries. The two worked weekend music jobs whenever possible and would often play for tips outside the refinery gates. In the mid-1950s, Clifton made his first recordings and began to build a local and Gulf Coast following. He eventually was recorded by Specialty Records from Los Angeles and scored an R&B hit with "Ay Tee Fee." Eventually, in 1956, he was able to make music his full-time occupation and had moved his base of operations to Houston, Texas, an important R&B center in the 1950s.

Chris Strachwitz, the owner of Arhoolie Records, met Clifton Chenier in 1964. He was immediately struck with the power of Clifton's mixture of French music and the blues. Strachwitz remembers: "I first met Clifton Chenier in a little beer joint in Houston's 'French Town' when Lightning Hopkins suggested that we go see him. Lightning introduced me to his cousin Clifton as a fellow from California who was trying to make some records. Clifton immediately suggested that we do some recording the next day! I was surprised when Clifton showed up at Bill Quinn's Gold Star studios and the duo of accordion and drums, from the night before, had turned into a five-piece band! I loved the sound I had heard in the beer joint where Clifton played the accordion and mostly sang in French patois, but he insisted that he sounded much better with the other instruments added and that he sing in English. He was obviously trying to make another hit like 'Ay Tee Fee.' The session resulted in only two usable sides which nonetheless got some radio and jukebox play along the Gulf Coast.

"The following year I returned to Houston and persuaded Clifton to record some raw Creole blues, two-steps, and waltzes along with his usual repertoire of R&B and jump numbers (Arhoolie CD 329). The regional success of the remarkable 'Louisiana Blues' sung in French finally convinced Clifton there was something very special in his unique Creole heritage. The following year we even invited his uncle Morris Chenier to play fiddle on his next album (Arhoolie CD 345), and the fine blues 'Black Gal' with funky fiddle and all became Clifton's best seller."

Throughout the late 1960s and 1970, Clifton gradually increased his visibility with hard rock work and more recording for Arhoolie. His popularity grew steadily as he became the leading exponent of what was becoming known throughout the world as

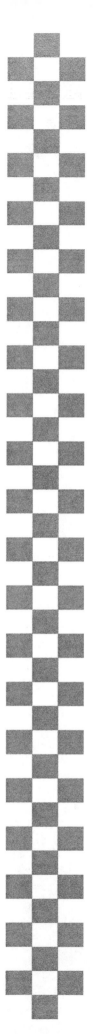

zydeco. In the process he became a fixture at blues and music festivals throughout the U.S. and Europe. In 1975 Arhoolie released his most popular album, *Bogalusa Boogie* (Arhoolie CD 347), which *Rolling Stone* magazine named as "the essential Chenier recording" for any record collection. About the same time, documentary film maker Les Blank produced an excellent film on Clifton entitled *Hot Pepper* (available from Flower Films, 10341 San Pablo Avenue, El Cerrito, CA 94530).

Clifton continued touring heavily during the 1980s but by mid-decade his health was beginning to decline. He died December 12, 1987. He was truly an original artist whose great talent taught the world about zydeco music. While he'll always be missed by those who knew him or heard his music, we're blessed to have such an extensive recorded legacy of his wonderful music to enjoy into the future. As they say in Louisiana, "Laissez les bon ton roulet!"

Dix Bruce

Sources: Arhoolie's Clifton Chenier recordings and Chris Strachwitz's writings and reminiscences of Clifton Chenier.

CONTENTS

Arhoolie Records • Down Home Music
Since 1960:

Blues • Cajun • Tex-Mex • Zydeco • Country
Jazz • Regional & World Music

For our complete illustrated catalog
of CDs, Cassettes, Videos, & more,
send $2.00 to:

ARHOOLIE CATALOG
10341 San Pablo Avenue
El Cerrito, CA 94530

To order by phone, call **toll free**
1-888-ARHOOLIE (1-888-274-6654)
or visit our website at
www.arhoolie.com

AIN'T NO NEED OF CRYIN'

(English Version of "Louisiana Blues")

Written and Arranged by
CLIFTON CHENIER

9

TU LE TON SON TON

Written by
CLIFTON CHENIER

* Bass in 4.
* Best shuffle is adding extra instruments: drums, guitar, etc.

I'M COMING HOME

Written by
CLIFTON CHENIER

JOLE BLONDE

Medium Zydeco Waltz

Written by
CLIFTON CHENIER

CALINDA

Fast 50's Shuffle Zydeco Rock (♫ = ♪♩³♪)

Solo & background riff

Written by
CLIFTON CHENIER

⊕ Play long basses, but do not connect to chords.

LOUISIANA TWO STEP

Written by
CLIFTON CHENIER

AY, AI, AI

Written by
CLIFTON CHENIER

LOUISIANA BLUES

Written by
CLIFTON CHENIER

BLACK GAL

Medium Blues in 4 (♫ = ♩♪)
Accordion Solo Intro

Written by
CLIFTON CHENIER

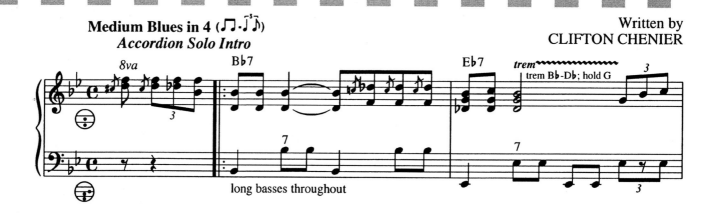

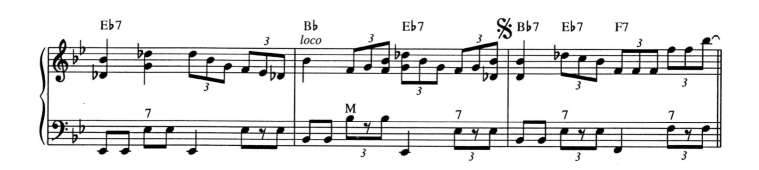

BIG MAMOU

Medium Zydeco Waltz

Accordion Solo Intro

Written by
CLIFTON CHENIER

I'M ON THE WONDER

Written by
CLIFTON CHENIER

Medium Minor Blues

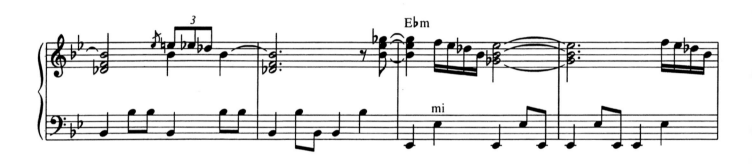

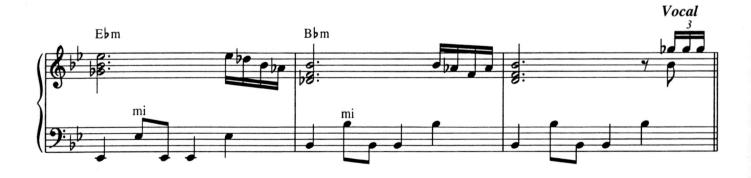

27

This page has been
left blank to avoid
awkward page turns

ZYDECO CHA CHA

Written by
CLIFTON CHENIER

I'M A HOG FOR YOU

Written by
CLIFTON CHENIER

Medium Shuffle Blues

ZYDECO ET PAS SALE

Written by
CLIFTON CHENIER

33

BLACK SNAKE BLUES

Written by
CLIFTON CHENIER